Spiritual
Warfare and Angels:

Stringe and Zate:
From the Darkness
--Into the Light

Spiritual
Warfare and Angels:

Stringe and Zate:
From the Darkness
--Into the Light

Cordelia E. Battle

iUniverse®

SPIRITUAL WARFARE AND ANGELS: STRINGE AND ZATE: FROM THE DARKNESS--INTO THE LIGHT

Work: Religious Fiction: Based-on-Fact: Youth novel-Christian Life. Characters, events are the results of the author's imagination. Factual information; events quoted from the Holy Bible [Historical-Fact].

iUniverse books may be ordered through booksellers or by contacting:

iUniverse
1663 Liberty Drive
Bloomington, IN 47403
www.iuniverse.com
1-800-Authors (1-800-288-4677)

ISBN: 978-1-4917-5578-5 (sc)
ISBN: 978-1-4917-5579-2 (e)

Library of Congress Control Number: 2015920673

Print information available on the last page.

iUniverse rev. date: 12/15/2015

"Scriptures quoted from the International Children's Bible, New Century Version, copyright © 1986 by Sweet Publishing, Fort Worth, Texas 76137. Used by permission."

Contents

Acknowledgements

I want to thank the Lord, for putting on my heart to write this, my first children's—Christian life-spiritual fiction book [based-on-fact]. I want to thank my family, for all their love. I want to thank the graphic artist, for adding the colors on the cover—I created.

Introduction

Two boys were best friends heading down the wrong road of destruction. However, each turned around early in life, before it was too late. Each boy had bad experiences that turned to good experiences; each boy is well able to help other friends. Other friends had experiences, but cannot understand what was happening to them. This is a fictional story about two friends that learned about good and evil, "spiritual warfare and angels, God and angels; [factual]." The stories are fictional, but based on true life situations— showing that God, angels, spiritual warfare and the Holy Bible are really true.

Note: I'm quoting some of the factual details [true] in this book, taken from the Holy Bible [Historical-Fact].

SCHOOL

Chapter 1

Let me introduce to you—Stringe

When Stringe was quite young, he went around with friends, taking part in activities, he did not understand. His parents went to church. He had to go to Sunday school that was quite boring to him, but he had to go. He started to learn about computers, and searched in other areas that were not good to watch, he did not let his parents catch him. He watched television shows that suggested violence, stealing, killing, hatred and other crimes. He got involved in watching the sexual scenery on the television and computer; "God created sex to be-one man, and woman-in marriage-in love; [factual]." His teen friends let him read their books about horror stories that involved "fallen angels; [factual]." He read as many spirited horror books that he wanted to read.

As he got older, he stole, hurt others, had many girlfriends and did not obey his parents. He started to experience things, he did not understand. He had bad dreams, and heard voices that told him to do bad things, not knowing where the voices were coming from. His thought pattern became confusing, because he knew all the thoughts was not his own, some thoughts were quite strange. He started being afraid, and did not want to go to school and sometimes, not even leaving his house. His parents began to notice different things about Stringe; he was staying more and more to himself. His parents decided to search Stringe's room, when he was at school, and found some of the books he was reading that talked about witches, darkness, evil spirits and death. A letter was found written by Stringe, and in this letter—he talked about not living anymore. Often wearing long sleeves—his parents was not able to see the cuts on his upper arm.

Then Stringe's parents called the pastor of their church and invited him to come to the house. The parents wanted to tell him what was happening to their son. The pastor knew about some of the teens in the neighborhood that tried leading some of the children into drinking, cutting and sometimes drugs. The pastor came back on a later day, when Stringe was home, and along with his parents talked to Stringe and prayed with him.

Stringe was not able to sleep at night and was afraid much of the time. He was watching television and decided he should change the channel. He saw a young minister talking about the Spirit Realm. He was teaching about creation, how God created all things, visible and invisible. Some in the meeting stood up that were close to the age of Stringe, and told their story about turning from a life of doing wrong things, and living in fear—to a life of hope and joy. Knowing that life on this earth sometimes being short, eternal life—looking forward; lesson learned. He learned that day from this minister and the stories from the others. He did not have to live in fear, always doing wrong things and being unhappy.

The minister gave the "Gospel Message about Jesus Christ; [factual]"—Stringe believed and prayed. He learned that he now belonged to God; he stopped little by little watching bad things on television and computer. Soon he did not want to cut himself any longer, gave up the horror books and gave them back to his friends. His parents told him about some good books to read in the future. Stringe was not afraid to go out his house anymore.

Stringe was able to sleep again. He learned how to rebuke evil spirits-"fallen angels; [factual]" out of his presences, "by calling on the name of Jesus; [factual]." He began to learn little by little that evil spirits [fallen angels] had no power over him anymore. He began to help other children in his neighborhood, and his first friend was Zate who he helped and became his best friend. He wanted to continue Sunday school and hear more about God and His Word. His life changed, he did not forget about his old friends. He sent up prayers almost every day, for God to help them.

Let me introduce to you—Stringe's best friend—Zate

Zate had an anger problem and got in fights all the time. These fallen angels put in his mind to hurt himself and others. He was quite interested in vampire stories and guns. His parents had a gun in the house. He was playing around with it and it went off, and the bullet went into his chest— just missing his heart. His father found him and took him to the hospital, just in time, before he lost too much blood. Zate stayed in the hospital for a while. Stringe went to see him in the hospital, but Zate did not want to see him. Stringe went back again and again to Zate, but he still did not see him. Zate got discharged from the hospital and he was able to go home. Stringe tried again, but this time, Zate saw him.

Stringe told him how God had saved him and he wanted to do the same for him. At first, Zate became angry, but remembered, he almost died. Zate began asking Stringe questions and saw he was a different person, not the same person; he used to hear others talking about—how bad he was. Stringe told him about "Jesus and the Gospel; [factual]"—Zate told Stringe, he had to think about it first. That night, Zate had a beautiful dream about heaven. In the dream a beautiful angel from heaven, "God's Messenger; [factual]"-told him that he did not know "Jesus as his

Savior; [factual]" and cannot see heaven. Zate woke up, not understanding what the angel was talking about, remembering what Stringe told him about Jesus.

The next day, Zate called Stringe and asked him to come over to his house. When Stringe arrived at Zate's house, Zate told him about the dream. Zate asked Stringe, if Jesus wanted to come into his heart and save him? That day, Zate asked Jesus to save him and come into his heart. He was sorry for all the bad things he had done. Together, Stringe and Zate were telling others about the "Good News that Jesus saves; [factual]."

CHURCH

Chapter 2

Stringe and Zate—new life

Zate went to Sunday school, but his parents did not go to church. Sunday school was for children and adults alike. His best friend Stringe went to Sunday school, along with his parents and went to church together. Zate and Stringe went to the same school—they both had several friends in the town. Zate was talking to his schoolmate and he told him how he really liked to play these real scary games on his computer. He explained to Zate, the games were taking up much of his time, and his parents were getting concerned about him. The schoolmate told Zate, he was experiencing a presence that was making him afraid. Zate invited him to go to Sunday school. Zate and Stringe were learning about angels in Sunday school, and sometimes shared what lessons learned-with their other friends at school.

One day, another friend told Stringe how certain shows on television he watched—when he went to bed at night, he had bad dreams and woke up afraid. Stringe invited his friend to go to Sunday school with him.

Zate and Stringe—go to the Sunday school teacher's house

One day, Zate and Stringe asked their Sunday school teacher—what is happening to their two friends at school that were having these problems. She told them that she was going to explain later, why their friends were having those problems. It was a small town and everyone knew each other. The Sunday school teacher did not live far from Stringe's house. Stringe's mother made a cake, for the Sunday school teacher. Zate came over to see Stringe and his mother asked them to take the cake to the Sunday school teacher's house. When the boys were at her house—she asked, if the boys wanted to hear a story? Then, she told the boys to take a seat and she began to tell them a story-sitting in her living room. The boys liked listening to her stories!

You see boys, explained the Sunday school teacher—you have learned how God created everything in this world that you see and things we cannot see. The boys understood what their Sunday school teacher was talking about; Stringe's mother talked to them about God and Angels. She explained that she was going to continue the lesson on Angels in Sunday school soon. She continued to explain-to them about Angels. She told them, there were good and bad angels. "All the Angels created perfect, until a high Angel wanted to take over the Throne of God. This high Angel [Lucifer-name in heaven] now called Satan, along with some other angels that decided to follow him, instead of God—was thrown out of heaven by Michael the Archangel—one of the mightiest angels in heaven. The day is coming, when the devil [Satan] and demons—all cast into the fiery lake forever and never hurt anyone again; [factual]."

The Sunday school teacher answered some of the questions about their friends. She told the boys, their friends needed to make some changes. She was going to explain, more to them in Sunday school class. The Sunday school teacher told them, it was getting late. Zate and Stringe left her house to go home.

Zate was thinking—about his friend

Meanwhile, Zate was still wondering about his friend that was spending too much time in front of the computer, playing games that later made him afraid. Zate asked his dad, why his friend was afraid after playing these games on the computer? Zate's dad told him, not to worry about his friend. But Zate did not stop thinking about his friend. Zate began thinking about the different Angels his Sunday school teacher told them, God created. Some of the things Zate and Stringe learned were, "God created all angels and some angels were messengers sent out by God—to help on earth. The angels cannot be counted; [factual]."

ANGEL

Chapter 3

Stringe and Zate—go fishing

Stringe came over to get Zate, because he wanted him to go fishing with him. Their parents told them, it was okay, but not to go too far into the water. When arriving at the lake, but couldn't wait to put their lines in the water! Everything was going fine, until suddenly, a wave came in and Zate fell into the water. Zate did not know how to swim. Zate began calling for help, but Stringe had told Zate, he dropped his hat on the way to the lake, and he went just a couple of yards to see if he saw it. Stringe was not nearby and suddenly, there stood a tall man who seemed to come from nowhere, and he jumped into the water and saved Zate. As Stringe was returning, he ran up to Zate and saw he needed help. He continued to help him out of the water, along with the man, not knowing what had happened. The boys packed their bags and turn to thank the man, but he was gone and did not see him anywhere around.

Arriving home—Stringe and Zate went to Zate's house, and explained what had happened. Stringe told Zate's parents, it was truly an angel who saved Zate out of the water. Zate's parents were happy that he was okay, but told the boys—no such thing as angels. The boys did not say anymore to them.

Zate and Stringe remembered what their Sunday school teacher told them about angels—are in your presence and you won't even know. The boys remembered to always be thankful, for God's help. Zate-prayed to thank God, for saving his life that day!

Stringe—tells his mother what happened—she explained-types of angels

Stringe later told his mother what happened to him and Zate. He told her about the man who came out of nowhere and saved Zate out of the water. Stringe wanted to know more about Angels and why God made them. His mother explained that "God created Angels to serve Him and worship Him. Angels are big and strong, there many Angels and cannot be counted; [factual]." She explained the different types of angels; [factual]:

"-Seraphim—Angels above God's Throne

-Cherubim/Wheels/Ophanim—Angels in the center and around the Throne of God

-Archangels—Chief Angels-Messengers

-Angels—Render service

-Satan—[devil]—Fallen angels—stripped of ranking— wicked forces [demons]"

-Note: "All of the above Angels are found in the Old and New Testament of the Holy Bible [Historical-Fact]."

Stringe's mother continued to explain, when he continues to study the Bible, having a better understanding and learning more about these angels. His mother believed Stringe about the man who helped them that day at the lake.

SCHOOL

Chapter 4

Zate and Stringe—go back to school

Zate was still wondering about his friend that was experiencing some problems from playing scary games on the computer. There were other friends who were watching certain television programs that made them afraid.

The weekend was over and it was time to go back to school. Zate and Stringe asked their friends to go to Sunday school with them the following Sunday. Their friends told them yes, because of wanting to see what it is like. Well, Sunday came and all went, except some of their friends did not want to go.

Stringe, Zate and friends—at Sunday school

The Sunday school teacher was telling the children how important it was, what stories you watched on television and computer. She let them know, it was also important, what books and magazines you read. She wanted the children to understand, about the unseen world that there were good angels and bad angels. When we do things that are not good, we become afraid. Looking at wrong things or reading about bad things, cause the bad angels to come into our presence.

But God wants us to do what is right. God has given us a guide, called the "Holy Bible; [factual]" to teach us the right way to live in this world. God gives us good angels to help us, when we do what is right. Sunday school was over and everyone went home.

Stringe's friend—talked to him the next day

The next day in school—another friend was telling Stringe about his sister that was getting into wrong things with another friend. He told Stringe, he heard her talking on the phone to someone; telling them she did not want to live any longer. He asked Stringe what he should do, if he should tell someone. Stringe told him he should tell his parents. The friend told Stringe, his parents did not understand and did not care. Stringe told him to tell someone he trusted.

Stringe did not know what he was going to do. When he got home, he told his mother about the girl who wanted to take her life. His mother explained, not everyone knows God and Stringe replied back that Zate's parents did not know God. Stringe's mother explained that good and evil exist in the world. Evil comes from fallen angels that want to make everyone do what is wrong—to hurt God. Stringe's mother told him to pray, for the girl and her parents to come to know "Jesus as Savior; [factual]." Stringe told his mother, everyone needed to pray, for Zate's parents as well.

CHURCH

Chapter 5

Months later—school was about to close

A few months went by and school was almost over. Zate's mother was in the market, and heard others talking, about some teenage girl who tried to take her life and she was in the hospital. When she got home, she told Zate what she heard about the girl. Zate right away, called Stringe his friend to ask him, if he had heard the news. Zate asked his mother, if anyone was willing to help the family.

Zate and Stringe—learn more-about angels

The following Sunday, Zate and Stringe went to Sunday school, and their teacher was talking about angels. She explained that when we listen and look at wrong things, it opens up our minds and makes us go down the wrong road by fallen angels. "The Bible shows us what we should not do and guides us on the right road; [factual]." Zate asked the Sunday school teacher, if fallen angels want to live in a person.

The teacher explained-how fallen angels give you thoughts that are not your own, and sometimes leading a person to carry out the thoughts—"every person has a free will; [factual]." But fallen angels [demons] really want to live in a human body and use that person to do evil deeds. The teacher told them the story from the Bible about a man who had many fallen angels [demons] in him:

> "This man lived in a graveyard in chains—he wore no clothes. He was not in his right mind and he was strong. He cut himself, breaking his chains and crying out all the time. Then Jesus passed by, and the evil spirits [demons] in the man knew who He was and became afraid of Jesus. "What do you want Jesus, Son of the—Most High God?—do not torment me!" Then Jesus told the unclean spirit to come out of the man. The name of the unclean spirit was Legion, because there were many living in the man. The Legion asked Jesus not to send them out into the abyss [bottomless pit], but to let them go into the pigs that were nearby. Jesus gave them permission to go into the pigs— about two thousand of them and the pigs went into the sea and drowned. Individuals saw that man sitting at the feet of Jesus, in his right mind and wellness. He told those in the entire city the great things, Jesus had done for him- Luke 8:26-36; [factual]."

The Sunday school teacher explained to her class, evil spirits are fallen angels and still attack everyone on earth today. If you belong to Jesus, fallen angels cannot hurt you. "Fallen angels are not afraid of anyone, but are afraid of God, Jesus and the Holy Spirit, and the prayers of Christians. Fallen angels are also, afraid of the good angels, because of their greater power. The good angels work for God [factual]."

Sunday school teacher—explained-about prayer

"That is why, it is important to pray and ask God for help. Prayer is talking to God in Jesus' name. Sometimes, prayer is just calling out—Jesus-help me. Prayer is also thanking God, for his help and telling God you love Him [worship]. We are God's children and He loves us all—that is why He sent His Son Jesus—to save us from our sins; [factual]."

Zate and Stringe—leave-Sunday school

After leaving Sunday school, Zate and Stringe ran into the brother of the girl who tried to take her life. The brother told them she was doing okay! Someone visited her in the hospital and gave her a Bible; prayed with her and she prayed the sinner's prayer. He told them that his parents were going to go to church after his sister's discharge from the hospital.

When Stringe got home, he told his mother—she was happy to hear the news. Stringe asked his mother to please pray for Zate's parents to get saved. Stringe explained to his mother, he understood that evil angels were as real as good angels. But when you belong to Jesus, the good angels watch over you all the time. Again, Stringe's mother explained to him, about being careful, what he was watching on television, computer and what he read, because good things you learn about, but bad things you learn about as well.

Zate and Stringe went out later and saw their friend, the brother of the girl who wanted to take her life. He told them, his sister is doing well and his family is going to church. He told them that his parents are becoming more involved in his and his sister's life. Zate was glad, because his parents are going to church now, and want to know more about God and the family is coming closer together.

ANGEL

Chapter 6

Zate's mother—a friend of the family was hearing voices

A couple of months later, Zate's mother told him about a friend of the family that was hearing voices. Zate's mother went over Stringe's house, and asked his mother about it, because she knew Stringe's mother was a Christian for a long time. Zates's mother knew that Zate and Stringe did learn some things about angels from Stringe's mother. Stringe's mother explained to Zate's mother that bad spirits (demons) try to get our attention and we should not listen to them. Bad spirits are trying to get everyone's attention, and wonder where the voices are coming from. Stringe's mother told Zate's mother, she was happy that she was going to church, and learning more about Jesus and the plans he has, for her new life. Zate's mother explained that someday soon, she wanted to help others in need of spiritual help.

Stringe and Zate—have questions-about spiritual warfare

Stringe and Zate heard that without God and not receiving Jesus, we have no protection from the evil in this world. "The evil is fallen angels [Satan & Demons] who hate God and everyone in the world, saved and not saved; [factual]." The boys understood about needing to learn more about "spiritual warfare; [factual]." The boys are now helping many in the community—to learn more about "Jesus and the family of God; [factual]."

Stringe and Zate remembered that our minds are where evil spirits attack, old and young alike, because evil spirits want to destroy everyone. "We are all in spiritual warfare, and we need Jesus to help us and protect us; [factual]."

Stringe and Zate—two families-come closer together and community

Stringe, Zate and their families became even closer. Both have open up their homes to help others in need of spiritual help, and anyone who wants to learn more about angels and spiritual warfare. The Sunday school teacher is still teaching each generation about angels and God in her class. The young are helping their friends to learn more about spiritual warfare and how to fight back with the Word of God. The two families, the Sunday school teacher and community have learned more and more about angels and spiritual warfare. Stringe, Zate and friends are helping each other, when bad things happen in their community. The boys knowing that in their community in the future—always someone in need of spiritual help.

CEB

ANGEL

Chapter 7

Stringe and Zate—want you to know

Stringe and Zate want you to know, no need of being afraid of evil spirits [fallen angels]. "Know that when you belong to Jesus, evil spirits cannot hurt you. You have the good angels watching over you. If you are having problems with evil spirits attacking you, call out to Jesus to save you. If you do not know Jesus, just pray this simple prayer and belong to the family of God today; [factual]."

Prayer—[factual]

Lord Jesus, I believe—I'm a sinner and I need a Savior. I ask you to come into my heart—and I thank you for saving me; In Jesus' Name-Amen

If you prayed this simple prayer—you were born again and have become part of the family of God—congratulations!

What you should know: [factual]

Spiritual Warfare—takes place in the mind, because it does matter what we think about. When you become saved, you have a better awareness of the things you are thinking about. First, knowing what is right and wrong, being aware and what we should know:

A. God gave the Holy Bible to speak to us and guide us.

B. Fallen angels [Satan]; attacks the mind, to take us away

from God and put us on the wrong road.

C. Our own thoughts—God created us with a free will—to

choose who we want to serve.

D. The following list—helping you in this Spiritual

Warfare:

1. Pray

2. Read the Bible each day

3. Read good books that help you

4. Don't watch scary movies

5. Don't play violent games

6. Don't read horror stories

7. Learn to tell evil spirits [fallen angels] to leave-In Jesus' Name

Final Word—[factual]

When you don't have Jesus, the attacks are greater by fallen angels [demons]. Fallen angels come with voices, cutting self, hatred, suicide thoughts, seeing scary faces, see objects on walls that are not really there, hurting others and more horrible things. Fallen angels come to attack in some of these areas and more, as you read in this book. But when you belong to Jesus, evil spirits try to attack you, but all you have to do, is call on Jesus. All power in the name of Jesus—good angels are with you to protect you always. In this world is spiritual warfare, but Jesus overcame, for us through the Cross. We have the victory over evil in this world. We cannot fight evil on our own. We need Jesus who has all Power and Authority over the visible and invisible realm.

There is a place, God created for these fallen angels [demons]; called hell [torment] and are going someday forever. God does not want anyone to go there with them. That is why, He sent His Son into the world—to save us from sin. But when we receive Jesus, He forgives us of our sins and heaven being our home someday.

Learning that you belong to the family of God, the good angels are watching over you to protect you 24/7. You don't have to fear anything or anyone! In this world, you have problems sometime, and Jesus wants to always be with you, helping you along in life. Remember, Jesus is just a prayer away and not letting us stay alone! Read the Bible and learn more about God, angels and spiritual warfare.

Stringe, Zate and the other characters were fiction, but the stories are true life situations. The Bible, angels and warfare in this world today is not fiction, but non-fiction. "I pray—to see you in heaven, okay!"

Scripture taken from—International Children's Bible:

Revelation 12:7-9—(The Angel, Michael-good Angel)— Then there was a war in heaven. Michael and his angels fought against the dragon. The dragon and his angels fought back. But the dragon was not strong enough. He and his angels lost their place in heaven. He was thrown down out of heaven. (The giant dragon is that old snake called the devil or Satan. He leads the whole world the wrong way.) The dragon with his angels was thrown down to the earth.

John 3:16-21—(The New Birth—God Loves You)—"For God loved the world so much that he gave his only Son. God gave his Son so that whoever believes in him may not be lost, but have eternal life. God did not send his Son into the world to judge the world guilty, but to save the world through him. He who believes in God's Son is not judged guilty. He who does not believe has already been judged guilty, because he has not believed in God's only Son. People are judged by this fact: I am the Light from God that has come into the world. But men did not want light. They wanted darkness because they were doing evil things. Everyone who does evil hates the light. He will not come to the light because it will show all the evil things he has done. But he who follows the true way comes to the light. Then the light will show that the things he has done were done through God."

Ephesians 6:10-18—(Wear the Full Armor of God)— Finally, be strong in the Lord and in his great power. Wear the full armor of God. Wear God's armor so that you can fight against the devil's evil tricks. Our fight is not against people on earth. We are fighting against the rulers and authorities and the powers of this world's darkness. We are fighting against the spiritual powers of evil in the heavenly world. That is why you need to get God's full armor. Then on the day of evil you will be able to stand strong. And when you have finished the whole fight, you will still be standing. So stand strong, with the belt of truth tied around your waist. And on your chest wear the protection of right living. And on your feet wear the Good News of peace to help you stand strong. And also use the shield of faith. With that you can stop all the burning arrows of the Evil One. Accept God's salvation to be your helmet. And take the sword of the Spirit—that sword is the teaching of God. Pray in the Spirit at all times. Pray with all kinds of prayers, and ask for everything you need. To do this you must always be ready. Never give up. Always pray for all God's people.

Colossians 2:15—(God has All Power)—God defeated the spiritual rulers and powers. With the Cross—God won the victory and defeated them. He showed the world that they were powerless.

Ephesians 2:8—(By Grace-Through-Faith)—I mean that you are saved by grace and you got that grace by believing. You did not save yourselves. It was a gift from God.

CEB

ANGEL

Chapter 8

Word Definition: [factual]

A..

God—Creator and Ruler of all

Jesus—Savior—Son of God—Head of Christianity [The Church]

B ....

Angel—Attendant-[give service]

Archangel—A High-Ranking Angel in-celestial hierarchy

Spiritual—Relating to God—[relationship]

Warfare—Military struggle—[two enemies]—Jesus disarmed the enemy at the Cross

C...

Good—Divine [God is good]—positive, excellent, righteous [free from quilt or sin]—moral [right behavior]—kind

Holy Bible—Collection of sacred writings—66 books—of the Christian religion—Old and New Testaments—[historical sequence]—men moved, by the Spirit of God to write

Prayer—Reverent petition to God—[talking to God]

D...

Demon—[Fallen angels]—evil spirits, following Satan [army against God]—But God has, all power over them all—still, under God's Authority

Evil—Wicked, corrupt, evil deeds

Fallen angels—[Demons]—banished from Heaven [thrown out]

Satan—Adversary, devil, evil, seducing humanity, demonic, out of favor with God—thrown out of Heaven

E ....

Believe—accept as true or real

Factual—Real, containing facts, based on facts

Faith—trust, belief, confidence

Fiction—Invented story

Grace—Gift of God

Non-Fiction—Real events

NOTE

NOTE

Printed in the United States
By Bookmasters